Just the Facts

Tobacco
Sean Connolly

Heinemann Library
Chicago, Illinois

© 2001 Reed Educational & Professional Publishing
Published by Heinemann Library,
an imprint of Reed Educational & Professional Publishing,
100 N. LaSalle, Suite 1010
Chicago, IL 60602
Customer Service 888-454-2279
Visit our website at www.heinemannlibrary.com

Designed by M2 Graphic Design
Printed in Hong Kong / China
Originated by Ambassador Litho

05 04 03 02 01
10 9 8 7 6 5 4 3 2 1

Library of Congress Cataloging-in-Publication Data
Connolly, Sean, 1956-
    Tobacco / Sean Connolly.
        p. cm. – (Just the facts)
    Includes bibliographical references and index.
    Summary: Discusses the history of tobacco, health risks associated with tobacco use, t
tactics employed by tobacco manufacturers, social consequences of smoking, prevention
efforts, and treatment options.
    ISBN 1-57572-260-7 (library)
    1. Tobacco habit—Prevention—Juvenile literature. 2. Tobacco habit—United
States—Prevention—Juvenile literature. 3. Tobacco—Juvenile literature. [1. Smoking. 2.
Tobacco habit.] I. Title. II. Series.

HV5735 .C66 2000
362.29'6—dc21   00-025653

Acknowledgments
The Publishers would like to thank the following for permission to reproduce photographs: Advertising Archive, pp.36,
39; Camera Press, pp. 5, 11, 23, 29; Corbis, p.10; Format, pp. 26, 31, 37, 47; Gareth Boden, p. 49; Hulton Getty, p. 22;
Magnum Photos/Ara Guler, p. 24; Magnum Photos/Michael K Nichols, p. 25; Magnum Photos/Ron Benvenisti, p. 27;
Network, pp. 8, 9, 17, 41, 45; NHPA, p .6; Peter Newark, p. 21; Photoedit, p. 35; Photofusion, pp. 7, 16, 33, 48, 51, 53;
Rex Features, p. 13; Science Photo Library, pp. 14, 15, 19, 30, 43, 46

Cover photograph reproduced with permission of Science Photo Library.

Every effort has been made to contact copyright holders of any material reproduced in this book. Any omissions will be
rectified in subsequent printings if notice is given to the publisher.

Our special thanks to Pamela G. Richards, M.Ed., for her help in the preparation of the book.

Some words are shown in bold, **like this.** You can find out what they mean by looking in the glossary.

Contents

Introduction

The public spends a great deal of time, money, and energy in its fight against the spread of such illegal drugs as heroin and cocaine. This is no bad thing, since these drugs—and others like them—cause misery, increased crime, and often death. But in this war on drugs, it is too easy to overlook some legal drugs that cause as much damage or more. Alcohol is one; tobacco is another.

Misguided notions of glamour

People have been fascinated by tobacco since it was first encountered by European explorers some five hundred years ago. Even then, it was clear that this substance had the power to keep people using it, no matter what the consequences. Some people criticized tobacco fiercely, recognizing some of the more obvious health risks associated with it.

Even today, many people are captivated by cigarettes and other tobacco products, and smoking is portrayed in movies and on television as glamorous and attractive. People who get caught in tobacco's spell find it hard to explain what keeps them smoking—some people find it relaxing, others find it stimulating, and still others need it to deal with stress. Whatever the reason, people who depend on tobacco to get through the day show textbook examples of **dependence** on a drug. The drug in tobacco is nicotine.

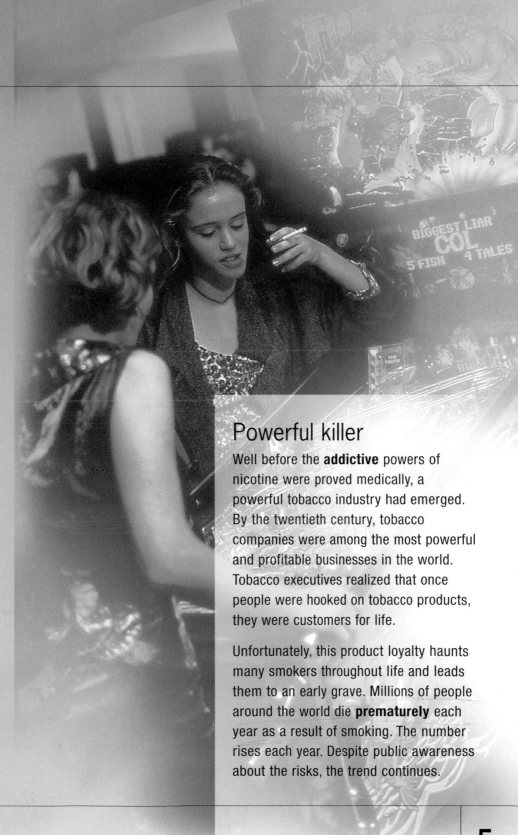

Powerful killer

Well before the **addictive** powers of nicotine were proved medically, a powerful tobacco industry had emerged. By the twentieth century, tobacco companies were among the most powerful and profitable businesses in the world. Tobacco executives realized that once people were hooked on tobacco products, they were customers for life.

Unfortunately, this product loyalty haunts many smokers throughout life and leads them to an early grave. Millions of people around the world die **prematurely** each year as a result of smoking. The number rises each year. Despite public awareness about the risks, the trend continues.

What Is Tobacco?

Tobacco comes from the dried leaves of the plant **genus** *Nicotiana*. The most commonly harvested species of this genus is *Nicotiana tabacum*, which is native only to North and South America. Tobacco contains nicotine, which is the drug that leads to **dependence** among smokers and users of other tobacco products.

Kinds of tobacco

Tobacco is **processed** in different ways and reaches the consumer in many varieties. The most common form of processed tobacco is the cigarette, which has dominated world markets since the beginning of the twentieth century. Different strains of the tobacco plant, coupled with varying techniques for **curing** the leaves, produce a range of tastes for cigarettes. In the United States and Great Britain, for example, the most popular brands of cigarette are described as *blond,* which refers to the lighter taste that comes from Virginia tobacco. Smokers in other European countries, such as France, prefer the darker flavor of cigarettes associated with Oriental flavoring.

Cigarette taste preferences reflect changing fashions as well as different cultural influences.

Tobacco farming is an important economic activity in many states.

In the United States and Great Britain, most cigarettes have filter tips. Cigarette filters are made up largely of tobacco stems and sweepings that are otherwise discarded in the manufacturing process. However, some smokers buy large quantities of unfiltered cigarettes or loose tobacco, which they then roll up themselves.

Why people smoke

Most of the effect of smoking is due to tobacco's active ingredient, nicotine. How nicotine affects smokers remains unclear, however.
People who smoke regularly do so for many different reasons, the most obvious one that they are compelled by a **dependence** on the nicotine, in the same way a heavy drinker is **dependent** on alcohol. However, smokers associate many psychological reactions with the habit. This suggests a range of other reasons for smoking, which are perhaps partly linked to this dependence.

The drug nicotine is classified as a mild **stimulant,** and so its effects would normally be expected to provide a boost in the form of extra energy and alertness. Smokers, however, note a range of other reactions to the drug. While many find that smoking is stimulating and makes them feel more creative, other people say that smoking calms them down in tense situations. Yet others simply feel that smoking distracts them from personal problems.

About 40 years ago, psychologists tried to unravel the complex mystery about the attraction of smoking. They concluded that smoking provided a type of **oral gratification**—simply holding a cigarette in the mouth provided comfort. More recently, theories about why people smoke have become more complicated, and many scientists believe that **genetics** may play an important role.

A dangerous habit

There is widespread medical agreement about the dangers of smoking. The health risks, which are discussed in more detail later in this book, range from heart disease to a wide variety of respiratory illnesses such as emphysema. Smoking can also lead to a number of cancers, most commonly lung cancer. Not only does smoking trigger these **fatal** diseases, it hastens the aging process. Many smokers develop facial wrinkles long before nonsmokers of the same age. Even nonsmokers can be at risk from the smoke exhaled by those around them. Inhaling smoke in this way is called **secondhand smoking**.

A choice of poisons

While cigarettes are the most common means of using tobacco, many people smoke cigars and pipes. Tobacco can also be chewed or sniffed into the nostrils. While users of these products often feel safe from developing lung cancer because they do not inhale tobacco smoke into their lungs, they often develop cancer of the mouth, nasal passages, and throat. Such cancers are often fatal.

Part of Society

Despite many laws designed to control the sale and use of cigarettes, smoking is common in most countries. Most governments insist that health warnings be printed conspicuously on each pack of cigarettes as well as on all advertising. Although many countries ban cigarette advertising on television, messages about tobacco products still reach the public. They appear in magazines and, more significantly, on the signs and billboards that advertise a tobacco product company's **sponsorship** of various sports competitions.

Early exposure

Children become aware of cigarettes at an early age. Even if their parents don't smoke, they encounter smoking on television, in movies, in advertising, and in public places. Despite the restrictions on tobacco advertising and widespread health campaigns about the dangers of smoking, children regularly take up the habit. For these children, the conflicting messages of concerned adults are no match for curiosity, boredom, and peer pressure. Some experts suggest that young people may naively believe that the health warnings apply only to older people. But they are wrong. Young smokers have an increased risk of both impaired lung function and respiratory infection as well as loss of fitness and prematurely aged skin.

A 1999 California study showed that at least 3,000 U.S. children between the ages of 11 to 20 become established smokers each day. Another study showed that in 1995, about 19 percent of thirteen-year-olds, 27 percent of fifteen-year-olds, and 34 percent of seventeen-year-olds had smoked within the previous month.

Put *that* in your pipe . . .

Young people are especially influenced by sports-related advertising. Stock-car racing, which is closely tied to the tobacco industry, is a good example. R.J. Reynolds sponsors a series of 33 increasingly popular annual races known as the Winston Cup. Its logos are prominently displayed on billboards, scoreboards, driver uniforms, and the cars themselves.

In 1999, to the dismay of racing fans, President Bill Clinton proposed restricting cigarette company sponsorship of U.S. sporting events.

Smoking Is Addictive

It is widely agreed that smoking is addictive. In any discussion of **addiction,** however, medical researchers prefer to use the word **dependence** to describe a person's compulsion to use a substance. Dependence, in turn, is usually divided into two categories: physical dependence and psychological dependence. A drug is said to cause physical dependence if the user needs to continually increase the dose to maintain the effects of the drug—a pattern called **tolerance**—and then suffers **withdrawal** symptoms when the drug is stopped. Alcohol and heroin are obvious examples of drugs that cause physical dependence. Tobacco, through its active ingredient nicotine, fits this description as well.

Studies have shown that people rapidly build up a tolerance to the effects of nicotine. First-time smokers experience a range of unpleasant effects, such as dizziness and nausea, but these effects lessen as the person continues to smoke. Sometimes, the unpleasant effects of smoking have disappeared within just a few days. Medical researchers studied smokers' tolerance for the stimulant effects of nicotine by giving a group of smokers equal doses of nicotine one hour apart. The heart rates of the group increased each time—one signal of a stimulant at work—but the increase was greater after the first dose than it was after the second. The experiment demonstrated that even in the short term, smokers quickly become tolerant to nicotine.

Getting hooked

Smoking, or nicotine intake, also causes a high degree of psychological dependence. This dependence builds in conjunction with the production of certain chemicals in the brain. Nicotine triggers the release of dopamine, a chemical associated with feelings of pleasure. But recent research has shown that over the long term, nicotine actually suppresses the ability of the brain to experience pleasure. Because of this, smokers need greater amounts of nicotine to achieve the same level of pleasure. Psychologists use the term **reinforcer** to describe a substance that drives an individual to seek more of it. This effect has been witnessed in laboratory rats, which will press a bar in order to obtain an increasing supply of nicotine.

Young people can become hooked on nicotine as strongly as adults can. A 1991 study showed that nearly two-thirds of smokers aged from eleven to fifteen said that they would have difficulty getting through a week without smoking. Three-quarters of these smokers said that they would find it hard to give up smoking altogether.

Often seen as less harmful than cigarette smoking, regular cigar smoking can also lead to serious illnesses.

Kicking the habit

Withdrawal symptoms play a large part in keeping people hooked on a drug. Nicotine withdrawal is unpleasant, and many would-be quitters fail at this first hurdle. Symptoms of nicotine withdrawal include an intense craving for cigarettes, irritability, anxiety, poor concentration, restlessness, decreased heart rate, and weight gain. Some people have argued that these symptoms really relate to stopping the activity of smoking rather than the withdrawal from nicotine itself. However, experiments have shown that the symptoms disappear if people get nicotine in another form (such as gum or patches). The symptoms remain if the same people receive a **placebo,** a product that resembles a tobacco product but does not contain nicotine.

❝I want to hurt something.❞

(Anonymous smoker experiencing nicotine withdrawal, quoted in *Buzzed*)

"Over the past decade there has been increasing recognition that underlying smoking behaviour and its remarkable intractability to change is addiction to the drug nicotine. Nicotine has been shown to have effects on the brain's dopamine systems similar to those of heroin and cocaine."

(The UK Government's Scientific Committee on Tobacco and Health, 1998)

Nicotine patches worn on the skin help some smokers to kick the tobacco habit.

The Effects of Smoking

By the time most people have become regular smokers, the reasons that made them start—thinking it is attractive or cool, or perhaps to try to lose weight—have been largely forgotten. Smokers gradually realize the short-term, negative effects of their habit. They find that smoking is expensive, it affects the way they look and smell, and it decreases their resistance to certain illnesses. Over the longer term, when smoking has become a way of life, smokers face the prospect of more serious, possibly life-threatening diseases. At this stage, the smoking way of life has become a way of death.

Smoking and appearance

Tobacco can affect people's appearance by changing their skin, body shapes, and weight. These changes are not in themselves life-threatening but they can, nevertheless, increase the risk of more serious ailments. Moreover, tobacco has a noticeable aging effect on the body.

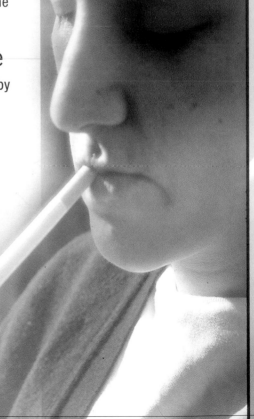

Advertising images such as that of the Marlboro Man are aimed at promoting a rugged, healthy impression of smoking.

Tobacco affects the skin in two ways. The smoke that is exhaled or that drifts from the tip of the cigarette dries the surface of the skin. Smoking also restricts the flow in the body's blood vessels, so that less blood flows to the skin. Some researchers suggest that smoking reduces the body's supply of vitamin A, which protects against some of these skin-damaging effects. Smoke-damaged skin has a grayish, wasted appearance. It has less elastin, the protein that keeps skin **supple.** As a result, regular smokers in their forties have as many wrinkles on their face as nonsmokers in their sixties. Tobacco is also linked with a much higher likelihood of developing psoriasis, an uncomfortable and unsightly skin ailment.

Smoking also affects the shape of a person's body. While it is true that the **stimulant** nature of nicotine means that many smokers are thinner than their nonsmoking counterparts, smokers' bodies store fats in unusual places. Smokers are more likely to store fat around the waist and upper torso. This can cause an imbalance in the waist-to-hip ratio (WHR), a measure of overall health. People with a high WHR run a greater risk of developing high blood pressure, diabetes, heart disease, and —in women—uterine and breast cancer.

The final stage

For many people, the only way to stop smoking is to die from it. The medical community has proven conclusively that smoking is the principal cause of some three million **premature** deaths in the world each year. Based on current trends, this figure could rise to ten million a year by 2030. One in two long-term smokers will die prematurely, half of them during middle age. Most die from one of the three main diseases linked to smoking: lung cancer, chronic lung disease such as bronchitis and emphysema, and heart disease.

The grim reaper

The deadly role played by tobacco smoking can be spelled out in a study published in 1999 by the American Cancer Society, the National Cancer Institute, and the Centers for Disease Control and Prevention. According to the report, lung cancer accounts for 28 percent of all cancer deaths each year. It also represents 14 percent of new cancer cases and continues to be a key force behind all cancer trends. Ninety percent of all lung cancer is caused by active smoking and exposure to environmental tobacco smoke. While male lung cancer death rates decreased about 1.6 percent per year between 1990 and 1996, the news was not so good for women. Lung cancer cases for women increased by 0.1 percent between 1990 and 1996, and lung cancer deaths during the same period increased by 1.4 percent.

Tobacco's History

The practice of smoking dried plant leaves is not new. The Vedic scriptures of India indicate that people were smoking various plants some 4,000 years ago. It is likely that some of these plants included tobacco, although not the same type of plant used today to produce cigarettes and other tobacco products.

The first people to smoke *Nicotiana tabacum*, which is the ancestor of modern tobacco, were the native people of North and Central America, where the plant grows naturally. The earliest real evidence of tobacco smoking comes from **artifacts** of the Maya civilization of Mexico, dating back about 1,500 years.

Meeting of cultures

By the time the first Europeans arrived in the New World about 500 years ago, tobacco smoking was common throughout all of North and South America. While Native Americans are often associated with the peace pipe and other examples of tobacco smoking, they also used tobacco in other ways. It was common to chew and even eat the leaves, and people drank the juices of the plant. The Carib people of the West Indies—who gave the Caribbean its name—wrapped small tobacco leaves inside larger ones before smoking them.

This mixture was the forerunner of the cigar. European travelers to North and South America in the sixteenth century noted these uses of tobacco and tried most of them. It was the different methods of smoking that appealed to them, and many returned to Europe with samples of the new plant. The Portuguese were the first people to cultivate the plant away from the Americas and to introduce it to the European public. During the 1600s, tobacco had become a cash crop throughout the American colonies. By the 1700s, smoking had become an important international industry.

Medicinal purposes

At first, Native Americans and then Europeans viewed tobacco as a medicinal plant. During the mid-1500s, tobacco was used to treat such ailments as headaches to the common cold. English and French **herbalists** guarded their specimen plants jealously. Sir Walter Raleigh is often credited with being the father of tobacco smoking, and there is some truth to this view. In 1586 he sailed to England from the West Indies with a large supply of tobacco. Raleigh's interest in the social, rather than the medical, side of smoking led to a boom in tobacco sales in Great Britain.

Ceremonial smoking of pipe tobacco was an established feature of Native American life when the first Europeans arrived in North America.

Taverns sold tobacco, as did specialist shops, grocers, and even goldsmiths. Not everyone, though, was pleased with this new habit. As early as 1602, an anonymous author published an essay called *Worke of Chimney Sweepers,* which compared illnesses characteristic of chimney sweepers with those suffered by smokers.

Growing trade

Despite increasing warnings about the dangers of tobacco use, the public continued to demand more and more tobacco. Virginia proved to have an ideal climate to grow the plant, and huge **plantations** were developed there to supply the increasing demand.

Up to the nineteenth century, pipe smoking and snuff remained the most common ways of taking tobacco in the United States and Europe. Cigarettes were introduced in Europe around the time of the Crimean War (1854–1856). British soldiers saw their French and Turkish allies with cigarettes, and adopted the habit.

The first cigarettes were hand-rolled, either by the smoker or by specialist manufacturers. Then, in 1881, the automatic rolling machine was developed. This machine produced hundreds of cigarettes in the same time it took to hand-roll dozens. Cheap mass production and the use of cigarette advertising led to a huge rise in cigarette smoking by the early twentieth century. During the 1920s, the first medical reports that linked smoking to lung cancer emerged. However, newspaper publishers ignored them for fear of offending the tobacco companies, which advertised heavily in their publications. Cigarette smoking reached a peak during the two world wars, when the U.S. government provided free cigarettes to allied troops to boost morale.

Hollywood star Humphrey Bogart, who glamorized smoking in such classic films as *The Maltese Falcon* (1941) and *Casablanca* (1943), died of lung cancer brought on by years of smoking cigarettes. Bogart, who had come to epitomize cool toughness, was only 58 years old.

❝(Tobacco) cures cancer of the breast, open and eating sores, scabs and scratches, however poisonous and sceptic, goitre, broken limbs…and many other things.❞

(Doctor Johannes Vittich in the early seventeenth century)

Public Reaction

The United States turned to producing and smoking cigarettes at around the same time as Britain, the early 1900s. Before that, most U.S. tobacco manufacturers had concentrated on processing tobacco for chewing.

The big boom

The popularity and huge sales of cigarettes turned the tobacco industry into big business. Individual companies became household names around the world. The big players in this development were companies based in the United States and in Britain. Some of the major tobacco companies, which are still widely known today, had their origins as individual shops. The biggest tobacco company today is Philip Morris, which regularly reports annual profits of $5 billion or more.

Cigarette manufacturers saw sales and profits rise regularly through the decades of the twentieth century. In the United States, sales of cigarettes reached a peak in 1960, when it was estimated that 40 percent of U.S. adults were smokers. Then things began to change.

And the bust?

Apart from signaling the high-water mark for U.S. smoking, the 1960s saw the first negative reactions to the tobacco industry. The public began to hear about research linking smoking with cancer,

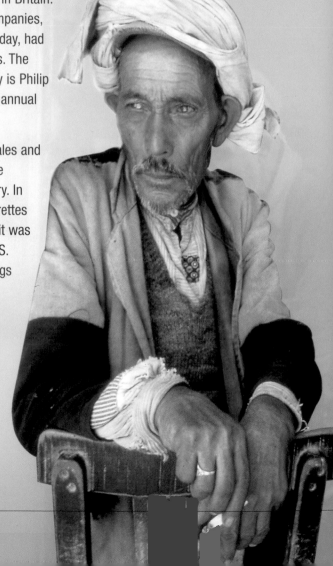

heart disease, and other potentially **fatal** illnesses. Other reports suggested that tobacco companies manipulated levels of nicotine—the drug that produces **dependence**— to keep people hooked on tobacco.

Increased public awareness about the dangers of smoking as well as **passive smoking** have led to many restrictions on smoking in public places. Detailed studies, such as a 1999 report by the National Cancer Institute, have linked passive smoking with lung cancer, heart disease, sudden infant death syndrome, nasal sinus cancer, and other diseases. It said that between 35,000 and 62,000 coronary heart disease deaths occur due to environmental smoke exposure. In **developed countries**, such as the United States, overall numbers of smokers have fallen dramatically since the 1960s. In the **developing world,** however, the story is very different.

THANK YOU
FOR
NOT SMOKING
AT
THIS COUNTER

Cigarette smoking is a way of life in many parts of the world, even if it is declining in developed countries.

Who Smokes, and Why?

Cigarette smoking is rightly described as an ugly habit. Nicotine-stained fingers, bad breath, stained teeth, constant coughing, and the smell of stale tobacco are disgusting, indeed. All these factors, coupled with the now well-publicized health risks, would seem to make a persuasive case for not smoking. However, people still do smoke, and young people are still getting hooked on tobacco. Why?

Government **public health** officials, medical researchers, and concerned antismoking activists have been trying to discover the factors that lead people to smoke and keep them smoking once they have developed the habit. So far, they have discovered that two important elements are age and **socioeconomic** position, what is often more loosely described as social class. The following information describes the types of people who researchers say are most likely to smoke, or *least* likely to quit.

Occupational hazard

There is a definite link between smoking and socioeconomic level. Well-educated people who work in professional jobs, such as lawyers and accountants, are far less likely to smoke than are less-educated adults who work in **manual** trades. Some 1999 U.S. statistics provide a clear-cut link between economic position, education, and smoking. While 11.6 percent of adults with 16 or more years of education smoked, 35.4 percent of people with only 9 to 11 years of education were smokers. And while 33.3 percent of adults living below the poverty level smoked, 10 percent fewer people living at or above the poverty level were smokers. Smoking behaviors differ between men and women as well. Since the early 1980s, cigarette smoking has declined by 10 percent for men but by only 6 percent for women. For whatever reason, the anti-smoking message seems to be lost on many less wealthy and educated people and on many women. Health policies must address this problem.

A smoker's day: What a drag!

Smoking is an all-day habit. One-third of all smokers have their first cigarette within fifteen minutes of waking up. Smoking this first cigarette is a ritual for the **dependent** smoker. Later, there are other situations throughout the day that call for lighting up. Calmed by the first cigarette, the smoker sets about his or her business, but remains constantly alert about how, when, and where the next cigarette can be smoked.

Many workplaces are nonsmoking, so the smoker will need to go to a special area—sometimes simply the office fire escape—to feed the habit. Smoking each new cigarette may be part of other daily rituals. For example, a person might always smoke with a morning coffee, after lunch, in certain social settings, or when someone else lights up. People will smoke when they are under stress or if they have just been through a tough time.

The smoker's day is punctuated with moments of panic when faced with nonsmoking situations, such as bus

trips, domestic airline flights, or meetings. Productivity lags as the smoker wonders how long he or she must wait before smoking again. A smoker's dependence on nicotine becomes painfully clear when the cigarettes have run out and all the stores are closed.

Across the Generations

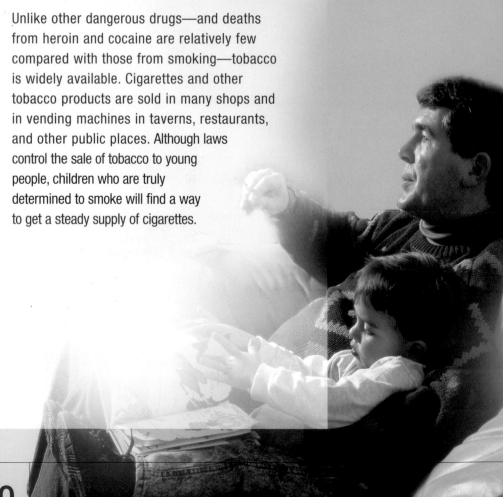

No matter how much people learn about health risks and the inconvenience and danger caused to nonsmokers, smoking remains firmly **entrenched** in most societies. Cigarette advertising has long since left the movie and television screens, but images of people smoking are still common. These images reinforce the message that smoking is cool, rebellious, or sophisticated. At the very least, they show that smoking, by its pervasiveness in our world, can't be that harmful after all.

Unlike other dangerous drugs—and deaths from heroin and cocaine are relatively few compared with those from smoking—tobacco is widely available. Cigarettes and other tobacco products are sold in many shops and in vending machines in taverns, restaurants, and other public places. Although laws control the sale of tobacco to young people, children who are truly determined to smoke will find a way to get a steady supply of cigarettes.

Powers of persuasion

More than for almost any other drug, a person's **conditioning**—or attitude about smoking—is developed in childhood. Very young people are extremely **impressionable,** and the actions of people around them are important formative influences. Children are three times as likely to begin smoking if both of their parents smoke. Almost as important—if less provable with statistics—is the influence of siblings and friends. Children are more likely to smoke if these close companions set the example.

The attitudes of influential adults, both in the home and in society at large, play a large part in children's attitudes about smoking. Health officials recognize that children growing up in households that disapprove of smoking are far less likely to smoke than those whose families approve or have no strong feelings. Parents who smoke but who disapprove of their children's smoking are in an awkward position. Their own credibility is threatened since they do the very thing that they are strongly warning against.

Advertising, which tries to manipulate public opinion, is quite effective on young people. One study of secondary-school children found that a minority of smokers (38 percent) but a majority of nonsmokers (56 percent) believed that tobacco advertising significantly influenced young people to start smoking. Other statistics show that children tend to smoke the brands of cigarette that are advertised most heavily. According to Philip Morris, which owns twenty brands of cigarettes, including Marlboro, one out of every six cigarettes sold worldwide was a Philip Morris brand.

❝Nearly 60 percent of kids who smoke use Marlboro, the most heavily advertised brand.❞

(The Campaign for Tobacco Free Kids)

Dangerous outcomes

Surveys indicate that the market for tobacco has become **saturated** in most **developed countries.** Tobacco manufacturers, like other manufacturers, are always concerned about increasing the number of sales they make each year. They realize that they must concentrate their advertising efforts on young people, in the hope that they will become future lifelong customers. The alarming U.S. statistics about the smoking habits of young people seem to be typical of other countries.

If today's trends continue, according to a World Health Organization report, smoking will kill five million of today's teenagers before they reach middle age.

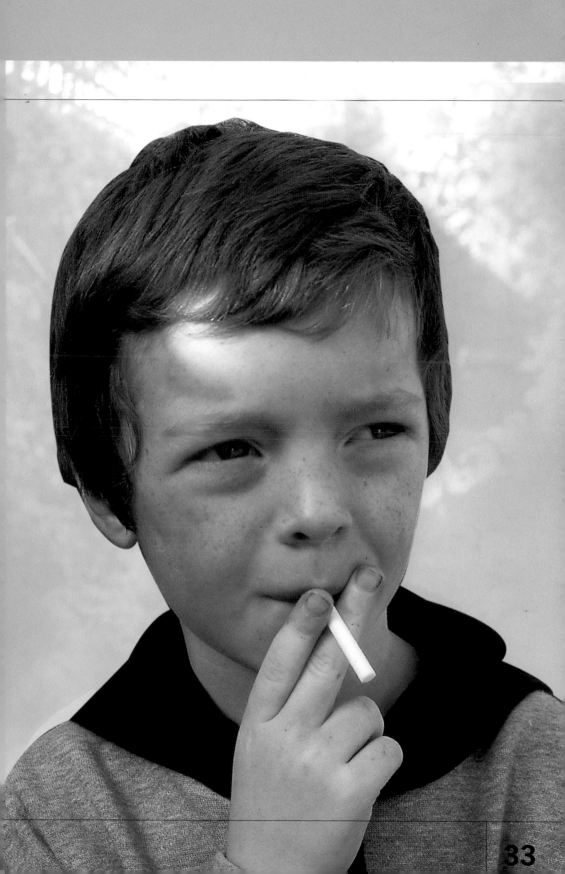

33

A Costly Habit

If health concerns about smoking aren't enough to keep people from smoking, the financial impact should be. The actual price of a pack of cigarettes—usually packaged in 20s—varies from country to country. Some of these differences reflect simple economics. The cost is lower in countries or regions where tobacco is grown and cigarettes are produced. In the prime tobacco country of Virginia and the Carolinas, for example, the price of a pack of cigarettes can be up to 40 percent lower than in it is in neighboring states.

Sin taxes

The variation in cigarette costs from one country to another is determined by the amount of **duty** that governments impose on the sale of tobacco. A proportion of the cost of each pack of cigarettes, cigars, or other tobacco products goes straight to the government. Sometimes these duties are called "sin taxes," since part of the government's aim is to control the use of a harmful product. Alcohol is usually subject to similar duties.

Many antismoking experts believe that governments now rely on these duties so much that they cannot make a genuine effort to crack down on smoking. In the United States, for example, tobacco taxes generate billions of dollars each year.

Disturbing arithmetic

Although most adults can afford it, the price of a single pack of cigarettes is still quite high. Maintaining a smoking habit, which will usually demand far more than one pack a week, is very expensive. By its very nature smoking is a repetitive activity, so frequent purchases are necessary. Taking the United States as an example—where the price of a pack of cigarettes in 2000 was about $2.50—it is possible to calculate the cost of smoking over one, two, or more years. A person smoking a pack a day, which is not uncommon for people who smoke regularly, will spend $912.50 in a year. Over twenty years the smoker will have spent $18,250, without allowing for future increases in price.

35

The Tobacco Industry

Tobacco is big business, and has been since the early seventeenth century when King James I of England combined disapproval with a keen business sense by increasing the **tariff** on tobacco. Soon, United States companies led the world in tobacco sales and profits. The present situation results from a series of mergers and takeovers, involving U.S. and British companies, at the end of the nineteenth century and the beginning of the twentieth.

Varied interests

Philip Morris, a U.S. company, is the world leader and claims about 12 percent of world tobacco sales. Its multi-billion dollar annual profits allow it to maintain its market share, either through extensive advertising or in savage **price wars** with competitors in the United States. Marlboro, the leading Philip Morris brand, is estimated to be the world's most **lucrative** brand of any product. The second largest international tobacco company is BAT Industries. As with Philip Morris, the statistics relating to this corporate giant are staggering.

BAT controls more than half of the cigarette market in

Like many other famous people, former U.S. President Ronald Reagan advertised cigarettes when he was a leading Hollywood actor.

I'M SENDING CHESTERFIELDS to all my friends. That's the merriest Christmas any smoker can have— Chesterfield mildness plus no unpleasant after-taste

Ronald Reagan

CHESTERFIELD *Buy the beautiful Christmas-card carton*

31 countries and produces nearly 600 billion cigarettes worldwide each year. Both of these companies, along with other giants such as Rothmans International, dominate the Australian market. In Australia, as in other areas, the companies have paid vast amounts both in advertising and in supporting research that tries to dismiss reports about the dangers of smoking.

The other factor shared by these tobacco giants is the way in which they have **diversified** their business activities. This is a common practice for any type of large corporation, but tobacco companies have additional motives for diversification. One is the decline or stagnation in the tobacco markets of the **developed countries**. Another is that increasing legal restrictions on tobacco advertising or public smoking makes the prospect of an outright smoking ban seem more likely.

Philip Morris and BAT, like other international tobacco companies such as R. J. Reynolds, Rothmans International, and Imperial Tobacco, have bought out a number of non-tobacco-related companies. For example, Philip Morris owns the large Miller Brewing Company as well as Kraft Foods. This combination of interests earns Philip Morris sales of more than $50 billion a year.

Targeting women

Despite their entry into other fields, tobacco companies have not totally abandoned their traditional markets. Like **public health** officials and antismoking campaigners, tobacco executives are aware of an overall decline in smoking in developed countries since **World War II.** However, in spite of this general downswing, tobacco executives have found evidence that women might be affective targets for tobacco marketing.

Since the 1970s, tobacco companies have aimed a large portion of their advertising at women. Some brands are even designed with women in mind. Aware that the proportion of women smokers had increased since World War II, tobacco firms portrayed cigarettes as a sort of **emancipation** for women. "You've come a long way, baby," read the advertising slogan for one of these brands launched during the 1970s.

The year 1972 marked the peak in the number of women smokers. While there has been a steady decline in female smokers since, the decline has not been as fast as it has been among men. In fact young women, particularly in the 16- to 20-year-old range, are smoking more. A major reason for this is sex appeal—the misguided notion that smoking keeps people thin. According to one 1993 report in a major fashion magazine, "So long as thinness is equated with sexual attractiveness in women they will continue to smoke, whatever the risks."

> **❝We also think that consideration should be given to the hypothesis that the high profits additionally associated with the tobacco industry are directly related to the fact that the customer is dependent on the product.❞**
>
> **(BAT internal memo, 1979)**

Tobacco advertising in the 1970s tried to link cigarette smoking with the promotion of equality for women.

In 1909, Mrs. Randolph Birch discovered that the laundry room was the best place to have a cigarette without her husband finding out. Mr. Birch suddenly discovered he had cleaner shirts.

You've come a long way, baby.

VIRGINIA SLIMS.

Slimmer than the fat cigarettes men smoke.

❝We can't defend continued smoking as free choice if the person is addicted.❞

(U.S. Tobacco Institute spokesman, 1980)

The World Market

The tobacco industry has other strategies to deal with the problems it faces in the **developed world.** Chief among them is the development of new markets around the world. The last 40 years have seen a massive expansion overseas. During the 1960s, the main growth area was South America. During the 1970s, the tobacco giants turned their attention to the Middle East, Asia, and Africa.

Target Africa

Africa has proved to be a real growth market for the tobacco giants. Sales there climbed by a staggering 33 percent during the 1970s alone. The marketing drive was fueled by advertising techniques that would never be allowed in the companies' home countries. In effect, the industry maintained that smoking builds brain power, physical strength, and social approval. One brand was advertised in Malawi—one of Africa's poorest countries—by showing a pack of cigarettes on the top of an expensive car. The message was obvious: our brand of cigarette lets you enter this exclusive world. Brand names used in Kenya include *Varsity* and *Sportsman,* which also suggest a world of glamour and prestige.

The tobacco-related problems faced by these developing countries are not limited to smokers. Local farmers are encouraged to grow tobacco, a plant prone to many diseases. During its three-month growing period, tobacco needs up to sixteen applications of fertilizer, **herbicide,** and **pesticide**. The next stage, the **curing** process, uses up vital and limited supplies of wood and other fuels.

Looking east

The 1990s saw a huge growth of international tobacco sales in the former Soviet Union and other countries of Eastern Europe. Residents of these countries have always been avid smokers, consuming 700 billion cigarettes a year. The major western companies are beginning to cash in. Companies use all sorts of techniques to build demand for cigarettes. One company working in Hungary offered free sunglasses to anyone who took a cigarette and smoked it in front of the publicity girl. The aggressive techniques seem to have worked. Western tobacco companies now control over half of the Eastern European market, up from only three percent in 1988.

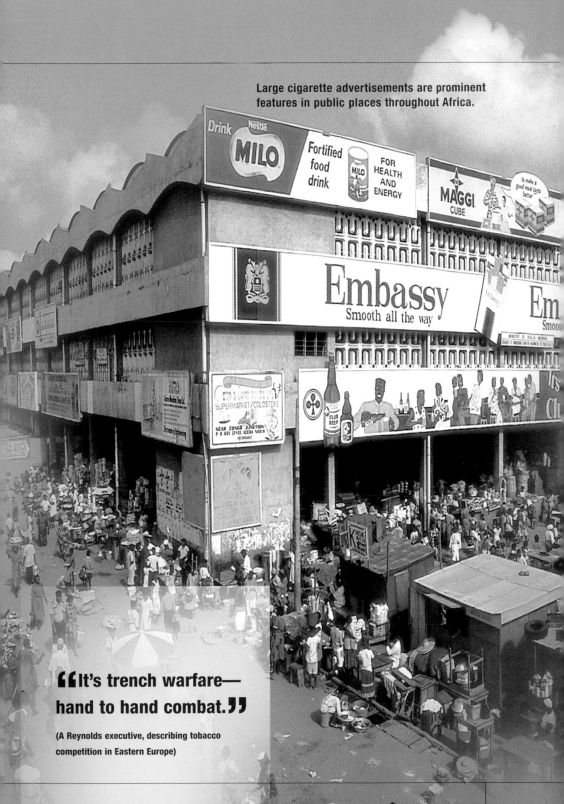

Large cigarette advertisements are prominent features in public places throughout Africa.

Drink Nestlé MILO — Fortified food drink — FOR HEALTH AND ENERGY

MAGGI CUBE — to make a good meal taste better

Embassy — Smooth all the way

Em Smoo

It's Cl

CLUB BEER

"It's trench warfare—hand to hand combat."

(A Reynolds executive, describing tobacco competition in Eastern Europe)

The *Other* Tobacco Industry

The tobacco industry generates billions of dollars in profits each year, as well as significant amounts of tax revenue for governments around the world. Smoking, however, has a number of other effects on the economy, and nearly all of them are negative.

Hidden costs

Industry in general loses a great deal of money each year because of the smoking habits of its employees. Most of this lost money is related to a decline in **productivity**, which results from whenever employees take smoking breaks or to **absenteeism** linked to smoking-related illnesses. In addition, there are the known side-effects of **secondhand smoking**, which can lead to resentment between smokers and nonsmokers in a workplace. In addition to these factors is the extra cleaning and maintenance costs that result from smoking.

A government bargain?

It is certainly true that the government profits from cigarette taxes. However, this revenue has a high price. The Centers for Disease Control and Prevention estimates that the direct medical costs tied to smoking totals $50 billion, or about seven percent of all U.S. healthcare costs. In 1993, hospital expenses accounted for 54 percent of all smoking-related medical costs. Other costs were for physician's expenses (31 percent), nursing home expenses (10 percent), prescription drug charges (4 percent), and home health costs (2 percent). Such figures do not include statistics about medical costs attributable to burn care from smoking-related fires, care for low birthweight infants of mothers who smoke, and treatment of disease caused by secondhand smoking.

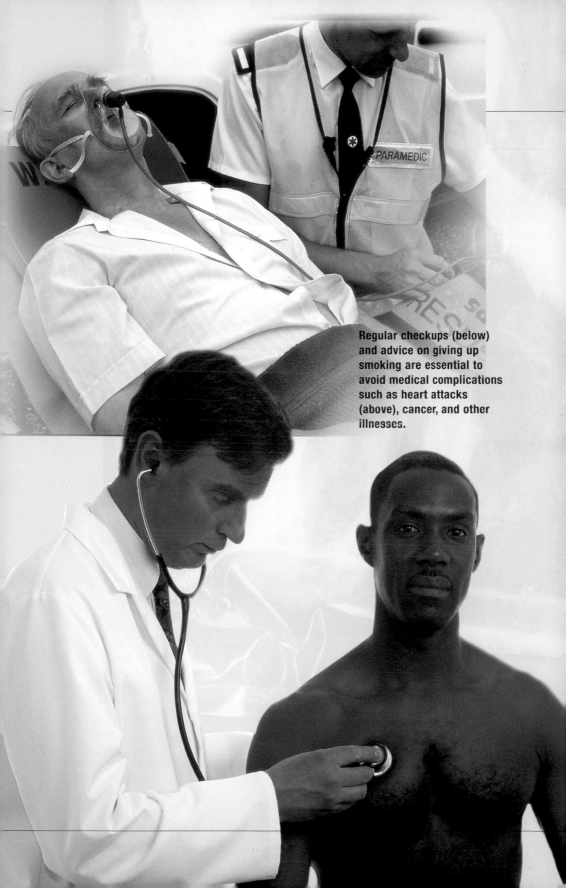

Regular checkups (below) and advice on giving up smoking are essential to avoid medical complications such as heart attacks (above), cancer, and other illnesses.

Legal Matters

In most countries, the tobacco industry faces many regulations controlling how tobacco products are manufactured, sold, marketed, and advertised. Most countries have an outright ban on cigarette advertising on television and in movie theaters. Cigars and pipe tobacco, as well as snuff and chewing tobacco, sometimes face fewer restrictions. The main thrust of most national laws is to control the spread of smoking among young people. The United States has long prohibited the sale of cigarettes to young people. During the early 1990s, many U.S. schools adopted policies of zero tolerance, which immediately and severely punished students possessing drugs (including tobacco products) or weapons or engaging in other dangerous behavior.

In the United Kingdom, it is illegal to sell any tobacco product to anyone under the age of sixteen. In Australia, advertising is strictly controlled, and all tobacco products must carry health warnings. In some states it is illegal to sell to anyone under 18 years of age; in others, under 16 years.

In the courts

The tobacco industry faces a potentially greater threat from **lawsuits** from individuals or groups of people whose lives have been damaged by smoking. In March 1997, for example, a U.S. court ruled that the Philip Morris Company had to pay $81 million to the family of Jesse Williams, who had died of lung cancer after smoking regularly for 43 years. About $1.5 million of this was compensation to the family; the rest was described as **punitive damages** because of misleading advertising about the risks of smoking.

In another **landmark** case, the major U.S. tobacco companies agreed to a $246 billion settlement with 46 states. U.S. Attorney General Janet Reno argued that for many decades the companies tried to trick the public into thinking that cigarette smoking posed no health threat. Secret documents written by top tobacco companies revealed that this was true. As a result of the settlement, all outdoor cigarette billboards were taken down, and the promotion of cigarette brands with cartoon characters and such gear as T-shirts and baseball caps was outlawed. The U.S. government used a portion of the settlement to create a national tobacco education foundation.

In Europe, tobacco imports, many of which come from the United States, face high taxes. This has led to a problem of smuggling. Recently, British customs officials discovered cigarettes hidden in a shipment of soccer balls.

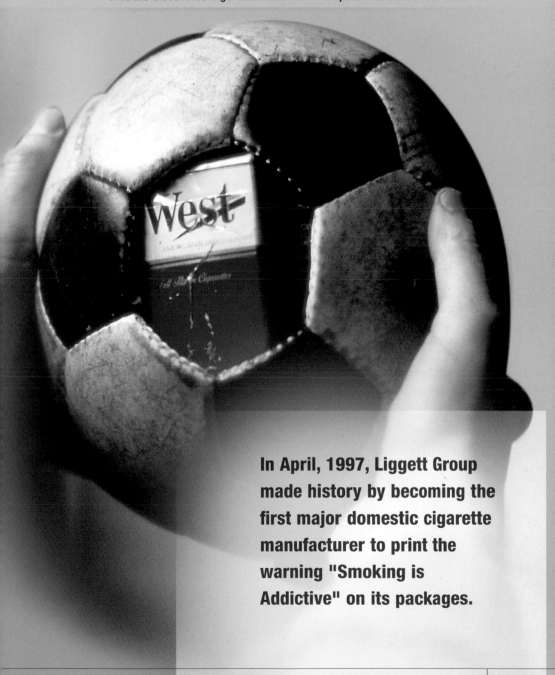

In April, 1997, Liggett Group made history by becoming the first major domestic cigarette manufacturer to print the warning "Smoking is Addictive" on its packages.

Treatment and Counseling

It is important to realize that smoking is a habit that almost always leads to **dependence**. Nearly every adult smoker, most of whom would like to quit, began smoking as teenagers or even younger. At this age, people should really be discouraged from taking up smoking, or encouraged to quit if they are already smokers. Willpower and determination underlie nearly every technique for quitting, but many people find it helpful to contact an antismoking organization for advice and specific tips. Many such organizations provide a helpful springboard for kicking the habit.

The youth focus

Karl Brookes is Project Manager with Action on Smoking and Health (ASH), an antismoking organization with links to similar organizations around the world. ASH is at the forefront of raising public awareness about all the risks related to smoking, including those that lead to death as well as non-life-threatening conditions. ASH can also counter many of the claims made by the tobacco industry in its efforts to play down the risk of dependence on nicotine.

"Young people are a special case," says Brookes. "We can spend a lot of time and effort telling them how smoking has more than 50 ways of making life a misery through illness and more than 20 ways of killing you, and yet they are often inclined to brush aside these arguments." This view is echoed by other researchers, who have found that many young people think of **fatal** illnesses as occurring only in adults. "Ultimately, we're trying to get the no-smoking message across and we're realistic enough to accept that the 'fatal illness' argument might not be the most persuasive to a teenager. The negative effects on appearance and the way smoking ages you are more likely to have an effect. And who would want to continue smoking after their boyfriend or girlfriend said they don't like kissing an ashtray?"

Quitting

There are many methods of giving up smoking, from hypnosis to acupuncture. Describing all of them would take up more space than is available in this book. Generally, though, they fall into two categories: those simply involving willpower or behavior and those that rely on special aids. Many of these aids take the form of nicotine substitutes that gradually lower the body's need for nicotine once a person stops smoking. They come in the form of nasal sprays, gums, patches, pills, and capsules. They either use the nicotine-reduction approach or have an additive such as silver acetate, which makes cigarettes taste disgusting.

People who choose not to use such aids often concentrate on dealing with the act of smoking. They see the rituals associated with smoking—the morning cigarette, smoking after a meal, and so on—as the main problem. Many such smokers quit by finding a replacement activity, such as sucking on mints or chewing gum.

The right frame of mind

Whatever approach people take, successful quitters agree that it is important to approach the task with the right frame of mind. It is probably best to find positive goals, such as improved health or **self-esteem**. As the initial difficulties ease off, such formerly difficult activities as running or hill-climbing, can be helpful. This offers positive reinforcement, as does the boost of spending cigarette money on more pleasant purchases.

ɭɭThere is absolutely nothing to giving up . . . there is no genuine pleasure or crutch in smoking. It is just an illusion, like banging your head against a wall to make it pleasant when you stop.ɟɟ

(Author Allen Carr, who formerly smoked 60 cigarettes a day)

Products designed to help people quit smoking usually provide nicotine in one form or other: clockwise, from top, chewing gum, lozenges, pills, skin patches, and a pen-shaped cigarette substitute.

People to Talk To

Smoking is an ugly activity despite the reputation it has for being cool. Like so many other drugs that lead to **dependence,** nicotine, in the form of cigarettes, takes hold of young people when they are most **impressionable**. And as is the case with other drugs, young people are not naturally drawn to smoking because it seems pleasurable. It is usually **peer pressure** that provides the first push toward smoking.

Other voices

It is important to overcome the temptation to be swayed into smoking just because you think it will make you as thin as a supermodel or as cool as a tough-guy film star. Try to make time to listen to other people about smoking, particularly ex-smokers or medical professionals. Their stories are very different from the glamorous image conveyed by tobacco ads and old movies, where everyone seems to have a cigarette dangling from their lips.

A doctor, pharmacist, or school nurse is a good person to approach for informed and confidential advice about smoking. Most of these people can outline the negative side of smoking in great detail, often putting it in a local context by referring to a neighbor or local resident who is fighting the effects of lung cancer or heart disease as a result of smoking.

Checklist of questions

Before approaching anyone for facts about smoking, think about information that might confuse you or for which you have heard only sketchy details. For example, you might want to learn about the risk of gaining weight if you stop smoking, or about the suitability of an expensive method of quitting. You could also ask whether a substitute habit would be useful. The answer to any one of these queries might be the jump-start in the fight to give up smoking and the road to a healthier life.

Information and Advice

Local libraries, hospitals, and health centers are the best places to begin looking for information about tobacco and about quitting smoking. Most communities have support groups for those who are trying to kick the habit. One of the best, most comprehensive sources of current information about smoking is the Internet. You can use a home computer or one in your local school or public library to access dozens of useful Websites relating to smoking.

Action on Smoking and Health
2013 H. Street, NW
Washington, DC 20006

American Lung Association
1740 Broadway
New York, NY 10019

American Non-Smokers' Rights Foundation
2530 San Pablo Avenue, Suite J
Berkely, CA 94702

Child Welfare League of America
440 First Street NW
Washington, DC 20001
(202) 638–2952
The Child Welfare League of America provides useful contacts across the country in most areas relating to young people's problems, many of them related to drug involvement.

DARE America
P.O. Box 775
Dumfries, VA 22026
(703) 860–3273
Drug Abuse Resistance and Education (DARE) America is a national organization that links law-enforcement and educational resources to provide up-to-date and comprehensive information about all aspects of drug use.

Foundation for a Smoke-Free America
P.O. Box 492028
Los Angeles, CA 90049

Tobacco BBS
(212) 982-4645
This site is aimed at specialists but has thousands of links to other tobacco sites.

National Center for Tobacco Free Kids
1707 L Street, NW, Suite 800
Washington, DC 20036
(202) 296-5469
One of the most influential international campaigners, with many resources aimed at young people.

Stop Teenage Addiction to Tobacco (STAT)
360 Huntington Ave.
241 Cushing Hall
Boston, MA 02115
(617) 373-7828

Washington DOC
P.O. Box 20065
Seattle, WA 98102
(206) 326-2894

More Books to Read

Ayer, Eleanor H. *Teen Smoking.* San Diego, Calif.: Lucent Books, 1998.

Condon, Judith. *Smoking.* Danbury, Conn.: Franklin Watts, Inc., 1989.

Hyde, Margaret O., and Dennis Kendrick. *Know About Smoking.* New York, N.Y.: Walker & Co., 1995.

Kranz, Rachel. *Straight Talk about Smoking.* New York, N.Y.: Facts on File, 1999.

McMillan, Daniel. *Teen Smoking: Understanding the Risk.* Berkeley Heights, N.J.: Enslow Publishers, Inc., 1998.

Monroe, Judy. *Nicotine.* Berkeley Heights, N.J.: Enslow Publishers, Inc., 1995.

Pietrusza, David. *Smoking.* San Diego, Calif.: Lucent Books, 1997.

Glossary

absenteeism employee's unexpected absences from a workplace

addiction physical or psychological craving for something, such as a drug; also called dependence

addictive causing physical or psychological craving for something

artifact objects made by people, not occurring in nature, such as pots, tools, or jewelry

class-action suit legal case brought by a group of people sharing a cause

colony overseas territory controlled by a powerful country

conditioning becoming used to something through repeated experience

curing process of drying of leaves to prepare tobacco

denunciation strong criticism

dependence physical or psychological craving for something, such as a drug

dependent relying on a substance, such as a drug

dependents people, such as children, who rely on someone else's income

developed countries countries such as the United States and Great Britain, whose economic systems have been established for many years

developing countries/world countries such as those in Africa, Asia, and South America, whose economic systems are new

diversified not focusing on one particular area or market

duty tax charged on a product brought from another country

emancipation to be free from the controls of traditional beliefs about a person's place in society

entrenched established strongly for a long time

fatal causing death

genetic characteristic that can be inherited from a parent, such as haircolor or even disease

genus scientific category used to classify similar plants or animals

gratification getting pleasure

herbalist gardener who specializes in growing and using herbs for medical purposes

herbicide chemical used to kill weeds that attack crops

impressionable easily influenced

intractability stubborn refusal to change

landmark court case that is a turning point in the practice of law

lawsuit legal court case against an individual and/or company

lucrative earning large profits

manual done by using the hands

mortality relating to death

peer pressure pressure from friends of the same age to behave in a certain way

pesticide chemical used to kill insects and other creatures that attack crops

placebo inactive substance used as a control in an experiment or to test the effectiveness of a drug

plantation large farm

price wars company's deliberate reduction in prices designed to force others out of competition

premature occurring before one would normally expect

processed changed in some way before being sold

productivity efficiency of a company or employee

public health area of medicine that deals with the welfare of society

punitive damages money ordered by a court to be paid as a punishment for injuring someone

reinforcer substance that establishes a need for increasing amounts in its user

saturated so full that it is unable to absorb any more

secondhand smoking inhaling the smoke exhaled by smokers

self-esteem sense of pride in oneself

septic infected

socioeconomic relating to a person's wealth and social position

sponsorship company funding of an activity, such as a sporting event, in order to advertise it and get publicity

stimulant drug that makes people more alert or energetic

supple flexible; easy to move

tariff money charged by a government on products brought in from other countries

tolerance body's ability to adjust to the effects of a substance, such as a drug

withdrawal negative physical effects of giving up a substance

World War II war fought from 1939 to 1945 between Germany, Japan, and their allies against Britain, the United States, and their allies

Index